Augustine

By Mélanie Watt

KIDS CAN PRESS

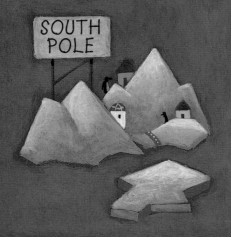

SOUTH POLE

ATLAS

Dad's important call

A.

SOLD

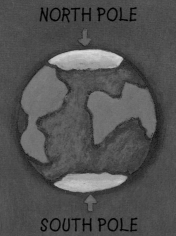

NORTH POLE

SOUTH POLE

My name is Augustine. My parents named me after the famous painter Pierre-Auguste Renoir. I live at the South Pole. But soon I will be moving far away. My new home is at the North Pole because my dad has a new office there.

EMPEROR KING
MOVERS

THIS SIDE UP

A.

SNOW
WHITE

In my bedroom, I gather all my toys. My mom says
it's just the tip of the iceberg. We also need to empty
the closets and pack our suitcases. I draw purple
stars on all my boxes. Moving is a lot of work.

I'm going to miss my room.

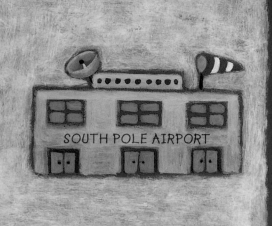

SOUTH POLE AIRPORT

We love you Augustine!

A.

First Name: Augustine
Last Name: Penguin

Augustine's suitcase

Now penguins CAN fly!

PENGUIN AIR

I carry my suitcase to the airport. When it's time to say good-bye, I feel sad. I'll miss my friends and my teacher. I'll miss my cousins and my aunts and my uncles. But I'll miss my grandma and grandpa most of all.

AIR SAFETY

A.

FISH CRACKERS

WASHROOM

occupied

Fasten your
seat belt

This is *my* first ride on an airplane. I play "Go Fish,"
watch a movie and eat from a tray. I look out *my* window
while *my* dad takes a nap. On the way to the washroom, I
see a passenger with his head in the clouds.

NORTH POLE
AIRPORT

NORTH
POLE

A.

INFORMATION

HOTEL

After a long trip, we finally arrive at the North Pole.
I ask my dad what building his office is in. I ask my mom
why I don't see many penguins here. She says I need to
rest because tomorrow will be a big day. I'm very quiet
on the way to the hotel. The snow reminds me of home.

1

2

FOR SALE
(great view!)

3

FOR SALE

8

FOR SALE

A.

4

FOR SALE

7

FOR SALE

6

FOR SALE
(reduced price)

5

FOR SALE

Today we move into our new home. We visited
eight places before finding the perfect one. Our new
house looks just like a castle. My mom loves the icicle
chandelier. My dad loves the hard ice floor. I love my
room up in the tower. It's cool!

Miss Linda's Class

Augustine's wish

12
3
9
6
A.

We love you
Augustine!

But at night, I can't fall asleep. I get chills just
thinking about my new school. Tomorrow is my first day.
I don't know anyone in the North Pole. I wish I could
turn back time and be in the South Pole with my friends.

Augustine

FROSTY
FLAKES

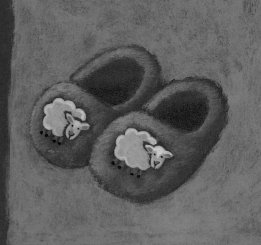

A.

ICY
FRESH

APPLE

JUICE

The next morning I hide. But my mom finds me.
I draw a picture of myself and show it to my dad.
I tell him that I have cold feet and can't go to school.
My mom says I should give it a try and hands me my
slippers. My dad walks me to school and wishes me
good luck. I think I will need it.

Miss Lisa

A.

When I walk into the classroom, all the kids stare at me and whisper. Miss Lisa, my new teacher, has a pretty smile. She introduces me to the class. But I freeze up. My accent is different. I'm too shy to say a word.

This is not my ball.

A.

At recess, the other kids have a ball. They are
laughing and shouting. It looks like lots of fun ...

I sit by myself in a corner of the playground. I'm glad I brought Picasso to keep me company. I draw pictures with my blue colored pencil. I think I will call this my "Blue Recess Period." Picasso agrees.

A little while later I notice it's very quiet. I see feet all around me. I look up at smiling faces. They belong to the kids from my class. I show them my airplane drawing and tell them all about my trip from the South Pole.

for Lenny

A.

for Lena

A.

for Felix

A.

for Selia

A.

Welcome
Augustine!

From
Miss Lisa's
Class

for Petula

A.

for
Harry

A.

for Oscar

A.

for Polly

A.

Back in the classroom, everyone wants to paint and draw with me. Miss Lisa encourages us to "express ourselves." She says we are going to have our very own art show at school next week. I can hardly wait!

Snow Peas

Iceberg Lettuce

Noodle

Soup

A.

Augustine Penguin

Snow   Cone

When I get home, I tell my mom and my dad all about
my new school and my new friends. My dad says that I
broke the ice with my drawings. My mom says she is very
proud of me. They tell me I will have some special visitors
at the art show next week.

petula

ART
SHOW
Miss Lisa's
Class

Polly

Lenny   Lena

A.

Harry

Oscar

Selia

Felix

Our art show is a great success. My new friends,
my new teacher and my mom and dad are there. And,
best of all, my grandma and grandpa have come to
visit. They tell me that the North Pole has brought out
my true colors. Picasso and I agree!

To John and Ginette

Augustine would like to thank the following painters for inspiring her:
Pierre-Auguste Renoir (A Girl with a Watering Can); **Vincent van Gogh** (The Bedroom);
Grant Wood (American Gothic); **René Magritte** (Decalcomania);
Piet Mondrian (Composition with Red, Yellow and Blue);
Claude Monet (Houses of Parliament, London);
Salvador Dali (The Persistence of Memory);
Edvard Munch (The Scream);
Leonardo da Vinci (Mona Lisa);
René Magritte (Ceci n'est pas une pipe);
Pablo Picasso (Self-portrait in Blue Period);
Lawren S. Harris (Mount Lefroy);
Andy Warhol (pop art portraits, Campbell's Soup Can);
Henri Matisse (Icarus)

Kids Can Press acknowledges the financial support of the Government of Ontario, through the Ontario Media Development Corporation's Ontario Book Initiative; the Ontario Arts Council; the Canada Council for the Arts; and the Government of Canada, through the BPIDP, for our publishing activity.

Published in Canada by
Kids Can Press Ltd.
29 Birch Avenue
Toronto, ON M4V 1E2

Published in the U.S. by
Kids Can Press Ltd.
2250 Military Road
Tonawanda, NY 14150

www.kidscanpress.com

The artwork in this book was rendered in acrylic and in pencil crayon.
The text is set in ICG Lemonade.

Edited by Tara Walker
Designed by Mélanie Watt and Karen Powers
Printed and bound in China

This book is smyth sewn casebound.

CM 06 0 9 8 7 6 5 4 3 2 1

Library and Archives Canada Cataloguing in Publication

Watt, Mélanie, 1975-
    Augustine / Mélanie Watt.

ISBN-13: 978-1-55337-885-3   ISBN-10: 1-55337-885-7

1. Penguins—Juvenile fiction. I. Title.

PS8645.A884A98 2006   jC813'.6   C2005-06797-7

Kids Can Press is a **corus**™ Entertainment company